RAINBOW MAGIC:
CHERRY THE CAKE FAIRY

First published in Great Britain in 2005
by Orchard Books
This Large Print edition published 2010
by BBC Audiobooks Ltd
by arrangement with
Orchard Books

ISBN: 978 1405 663854

HiT entertainment

British Library Cataloguing in Publication Data available

BBC 4·12·09

Cherry
the Cake
Fairy

Daisy Meadows

Illustrated by Georgie Ripper

The Fairyland Palace

Clearing

The Village Hall

Twisty Lane

Wetherbury Village

A Very Special
Party Invitation

Our gracious King and gentle Queen
Are loved by fairies all.
One thousand years have they ruled well,
Through troubles great and small.

In honour of their glorious reign
A party has been planned,
To celebrate their jubilee
Throughout all Fairyland.

The party is a royal surprise,
We hope they'll be delighted.
So shine your wand and press your dress...
For *you* have been invited!

RSVP: HRH THE FAIRY GODMOTHER

BBC 4·12·09

Contents

For Saoirse Medway

Special thanks to
Sue Mongredien

A Birthday Surprise

"I just know this is going to be
a wonderful birthday!" Kirsty Tate
exclaimed happily, her eyes shining.

Mrs Tate laughed across the
breakfast table. "You've only been
awake for half an hour, Kirsty,"
she said.

"I know," Kirsty replied. "But look
at all these cards I've been sent!

1

And there's my party this afternoon. And best of all, Rachel's here for a whole week!" She grinned at her best friend, Rachel Walker, who was sitting next to her.

The two girls were spending a week of the Easter holidays together. They had met on holiday the year before and, since then, they had had all kinds of magical adventures together. First, they had helped all seven of the Rainbow Fairies return to Fairyland. Then, they'd helped the Weather Fairies stop wicked Jack Frost from causing weather chaos!

The girls finished their breakfast and went to get dressed. Rachel was

2

halfway up the stairs behind Kirsty, when she noticed another envelope coming through the letterbox. She ran to get it. It was a very grand-looking, sparkly gold envelope, and it felt heavy in her hand. She glanced at the front curiously – and then gasped in surprise.

Miss Kirsty Tate and *Miss Rachel Walker*, the beautiful loopy handwriting read. Rachel blinked. A card for Kirsty or her? It wasn't her birthday for another three months!

She raced up the stairs, two at a time, puzzling it over. She didn't recognise the handwriting, so it couldn't be from her mum or dad. But who else knew that she was staying with Kirsty?

"Look," cried Rachel, bursting into Kirsty's bedroom. "Another card – and it's for both of us!"

Kirsty took the envelope and

gently turned it over, running her finger around the red wax seal on the back. "You open it," she said, passing the letter back to Rachel. "I've had all my other cards this morning."

Rachel's fingers trembled with excitement as she carefully broke the wax seal. As soon as the envelope was open, glittering clouds of fairy dust billowed into the air, followed by a rainbow of colour that soared across the room.

Both girls stared, open-mouthed.
Riding on top of the rainbow, just as
if he was surfing on a wave, was
Bertram, the Fairyland frog
footman! Rachel and Kirsty had met
him before in their fairy adventures.
But they hadn't expected to see him
again in Kirsty's bedroom.

Bertram hopped off the rainbow onto Kirsty's chest of drawers and bowed deeply. He wore a red waistcoat and carried a gold bugle.

Kirsty grabbed Rachel's hand excitedly and squeezed it. She couldn't help wondering if this would be the start of another magical quest!

Bertram tooted on the bugle, then pulled a tiny scroll from one of his pockets. He unrolled it, and cleared his throat. "Ahem. It is with great pleasure," he began, "that I bring you good news. The Fairy Godmother hereby invites Kirsty Tate and Rachel Walker to a surprise party – for the Fairy King and Queen's 1000th jubilee!"

"Wow!" gasped Rachel.

"Yes, please!" Kirsty cried.

From another of his pockets, Bertram pulled out a tiny bag of fairy dust and began sprinkling it over Kirsty's mirror. As the girls watched, the mirror's reflection vanished and a whole new scene appeared before their eyes.

"It's Fairyland!" Rachel breathed, leaning closer for a better look.

"Correct," said Bertram. "The Fairy Party Workshop, to be precise. All the Party Fairies have been working very hard to make sure the King and Queen's party is absolutely perfect."

Kirsty and Rachel gazed in delight at the small figures they could see bustling around in the workshop.

"There's Cherry the Cake Fairy,
making a special party cake,"
Bertram told them, pointing
a webbed green finger.
The cake did indeed
look wonderful. It
was shaped like
a fairy palace and
it sparkled with
magic. "That's
Grace the Glitter
Fairy, making
lots of magical
decorations. And
can you see the
fairy wrapping up
gifts so prettily?
She's Jasmine
the Present Fairy."
 The two girls watched in
delight as Jasmine tied a pink
satin bow around one of the presents.

"Who else is there?" Kirsty asked eagerly.

Bertram pointed. "There's Polly the Party Fun Fairy. She's in charge of party games. And Melodie the Music Fairy sorts out the best party tunes. She's teaching the fairy orchestra how to play the harmonies for 'Happy Jubilee'." The girls fell silent and listened to the sweet sounds of fairy music tinkling through the mirror. "It's gorgeous," Rachel sighed.

Bertram went on. "Honey the Sweet Fairy is making sure there are enough treats to go round, and

Phoebe the Fashion Fairy – she's the one with the extra-sparkly wings, look – is in charge of everybody's party outfits."

Kirsty gazed in wonder at the beautiful dress Phoebe was working

on. It was covered with hundreds of sequins and jewels that glittered in the light. "It's lovely," breathed Kirsty, her eyes wide with excitement. "And we're really invited to the party?"

"Oh, yes," Bertram replied. "The

Fairy Godmother says that you and
Rachel will be special guests."

"Special guests!" Rachel echoed,
looking thrilled at the thought.

"So, when is the party?
And how will
we get there?"
Kirsty asked.

Bertram
murmured
something at
the mirror
and the
Fairyland
scene
dissolved into
hundreds of
twinkling stars,
before finally disappearing. "The
party's at the end of the week. And
the Fairy Godmother will send
a magic rainbow to collect you,"

he said. He handed the magic invitation to Rachel. "To get to Fairyland, all you have to do is step into the end of the rainbow," he explained, "like this."

Kirsty and Rachel watched as Bertram placed one froggy foot, then another, into the colourful rainbow that hovered in the air. And then – *whoosh* – with a shower of golden fairy dust, he was gone.

"Hurrah!" exclaimed Kirsty. "I knew this was going to be a brilliant birthday."

Fun and Games

Rachel and Kirsty got dressed, chatting excitedly.

"'Special guests', the Fairy Godmother called us," Rachel said proudly, tying up her hair in a band. "Imagine! You and me, special guests of the Fairy King and Queen!"

"It's amazing," Kirsty grinned,

brushing her hair. "I can't wait
to go to Fairyland again."

Just then, there was a shout from
downstairs. "Come on, girls!"
Mrs Tate called. "There's lots to
do before the party starts."

Rachel and Kirsty looked at each
other in amazement. How did
Mrs Tate know about the Fairyland
party? Then Kirsty chuckled. "She
means my party," she said. "Do
you know, I'd almost forgotten
all about it!"

The girls laughed and hurried

downstairs. In the kitchen, Mr Tate was icing Kirsty's birthday cake. "There," he said, putting nine candles on top. "It's all finished."

"That looks delicious, Dad," Kirsty said, hugging him. "Come on, Rachel – let's see what Mum wants us to do."

Mrs Tate soon had the two girls making up party bags for all of Kirsty's guests. Then they blew up lots of pink and lilac balloons to hang from the ceiling. And finally there was just time for the girls to put on their party dresses before the guests arrived.

"Musical Statues first," Mrs Tate

announced to all the girls gathered in the lounge. "When the music stops – so do you!"

The music started and everybody danced. Then Mr Tate switched it off – and everybody froze on the spot. Rachel was standing on one leg, trying to keep as still as possible, when she suddenly saw swirls of red and purple glitter floating through the doorway. She stared in surprise, wondering what it could be. Then she flicked her eyes to the side, wondering if Kirsty had spotted the glitter, too. Kirsty's startled expression told Rachel that she had, but none of the other children seemed to have noticed anything unusual.

The sparkling dust floated up to Rachel, drifting right under her nose. "Atishoo! Atishoo! Atishoo!" she sneezed.

Now the dust was under Kirsty's nose, too. It was so ticklish, she just couldn't help rubbing her nose.

"Rachel and Kirsty – you two are out!" Mrs Tate said. "Here comes the music again."

As quickly as they had appeared, the swirls of red and purple glitter vanished. Rachel frowned at Kirsty. "What was that?" she hissed as they went to sit down.

Kirsty grabbed her arm and steered her towards the door.

"I think it might have had something to do with her," she whispered, pointing through the doorway.

Rachel followed Kirsty's finger, and a broad smile spread over her face. For there, hovering in mid-air and waving at the girls, was a tiny sparkling fairy!

Stop Thief!

"You're one of the Party Fairies!"
Rachel exclaimed as they rushed
over to speak to the fairy. "We saw
you in Bertram's picture."

The fairy smiled. She had lovely,
deep violet eyes and long, dark,
curly hair, tied in bunches with red
ribbons. She wore a red skirt, a pink
wrap-around top, red party shoes
and stripy socks. From her wrist,

swung a sparkly red party bag.
"I certainly am," she replied, with
a little curtsey. "I'm Cherry the
Cake Fairy."

An anxious
frown creased
her forehead.
"I'm sorry if
my fairy dust
spoiled your
game," she
went on, "but
I really need your help!"

"Of course!" Kirsty said at once.

"Whatever's happened?" Rachel
asked.

Cherry smiled gratefully. "Well,
you see, as the Cake Fairy, whenever
a party is in danger of being ruined
by a spoiled cake, I get called away
from Fairyland to fix it. And today,
I've been very busy. One of Jack

Frost's goblins has been spoiling birthday cakes all over the country. He steals the cake candles, and stomps in the icing." She bit her lip. "And he's on his way to Kirsty's party right now!"

Rachel's mouth fell open. "What a cheek!" she exclaimed.

Kirsty glanced over to the kitchen door. "Why is the goblin spoiling all the cakes?" she asked. "And what can we do to stop him?"

Cherry's eyes flashed. "Nobody knows what the goblin is up to," she told the girls. "But one thing's for sure – if Jack Frost's behind it, it's bound to be something bad." She shrugged. "All we can do is try to catch the goblin before he causes any more trouble."

"What are we waiting for?" Rachel cried. "Let's stand guard over Kirsty's cake at once!"

The girls raced to the kitchen, with Cherry fluttering along behind. As soon as they opened the kitchen door, though, they knew that they were too late. All the candles had been pulled out of Kirsty's cake, and there were goblin footprints in the icing.

"Oh, no!" cried Kirsty in dismay. "He's ruined it!"

"He's taken all the candles, too,"
Rachel added crossly.

"And I'll take this, as well!" they
heard somebody cackle. And before
anyone could stop him, a grinning
green goblin jumped out from
behind one of the table legs,
snatched Cherry's party bag out
of her hands and ran off,
laughing nastily.

A Tricky Problem

"Hey!" Cherry cried. "Give that back!"

Kirsty and Rachel stared in horror as the goblin ran away. He was his normal size, Rachel noted with relief. She remembered that the Fairy King and Queen had taken Jack Frost's magic away for one year, after his mean mischief had nearly ruined Christmas. Clearly, his punishment meant that he hadn't been able to cast a spell to make the goblins super-sized like he'd done once before. An enormous rucksack bumped up and down on the goblin's back. It was stuffed full of party candles.

"We've got to get my party bag back!" Cherry cried, flying after the thief. "Quick!"

The goblin was just about to dodge out of the kitchen door, when Kirsty's kitten, Pearl, came bounding into the room. As soon as Pearl saw the goblin, she fluffed up her black and white fur in alarm and hissed.

The goblin's eyes bulged in panic and he skidded to a halt. Then he climbed up to one of the kitchen cupboards and locked himself in!

Cherry flitted about anxiously. "That party bag has got all my magical fairy dust inside," she fretted. "I need that to help make parties perfect – and to finish off the King and Queen's jubilee cake."

Rachel banged on the cupboard door. "Give that party bag back to Cherry this minute!" she ordered the goblin.

"No chance," the goblin shouted back sulkily. "It's mine now – and as soon as I get out of here, I'll be giving it to Jack Frost."

"What does he want it for?" Kirsty asked curiously. The goblin gave a gloating chuckle. "For his party of course," he replied. "The King and Queen said he's got to stay in his ice castle, but they didn't say he couldn't have a party – and a very grand one it's going to be, too! Now that I've got this party bag of magic dust, his cake is going to be the most splendid cake you ever saw." There was another cackle of glee from the cupboard. "Just you wait – once we've got all the Party Fairies' party bags, Jack Frost will use the magic dust, instead of his own magic, to make his party extra-special."

Cherry had turned quite pale. She beckoned the girls back over to the table, where they huddled together to hear her whisper.

"It's bad enough that he's got my party bag when I haven't finished the King and Queen's cake," she said. "But if the goblins are planning to steal all the magical party bags, then none of the Party Fairies will be able to finish their work in time for the jubilee."

She shook her head miserably. "The surprise party will be ruined!"

A Sticky Solution

The girls thought hard to try and find a way of recovering Cherry's party bag. But they couldn't think of anything.

"The Fairy Godmother is much more powerful than a goblin," Cherry sighed. "She'd soon sort all this out if only I could get the goblin back to Fairyland. But I can't magic him there while he's in that cupboard – or while he's running away. I need him to keep fairly still, so that I can wave my wand over him."

Kirsty found her gaze drifting towards her ruined birthday cake. "Poor Dad spent ages on that icing," she said sadly.

Then she grinned suddenly as a thought struck her. "That's it!" she muttered. "That's how we'll catch him out!"

"How?" Rachel asked blankly.

"We need to make more icing for this cake," Kirsty said loudly. She took out a box of icing sugar and started mixing some icing in a bowl. Then she added quietly, "Cherry, could

you use some fairy magic to make
this icing extra-sticky?"

"No problem," Cherry replied.

She waved her
wand over the
bowl and a
stream of
sparkling
purple and red
fairy dust
swirled around it.
The white icing
glittered for a split-second and
strange red and purple sparks
crackled above it. Then it turned
a glossy white again.

Kirsty gave one last stir and
smiled. "Super-sticky!" she
whispered.

Rachel was still frowning.
"I don't—" she began.

But Kirsty put a finger to her lips.

"It's a trap!" she whispered into Rachel's ear. Quickly, she covered the cake with the new icing. "We'd better get back to the party now that the cake's all right again. We'll just leave it here on the table..." she said loudly.

Rachel and Cherry followed Kirsty out of the room. Holding their breath, they waited outside the kitchen, peeping through the crack in the door to see if Kirsty's trap would work.

Sure enough, after a moment, the cupboard door creaked open and the goblin climbed down and skipped gleefully across the floor. Grinning nastily, he climbed up onto the kitchen table, and then made a massive leap straight onto the top of the newly-iced cake.

"There he goes," Kirsty whispered
to Rachel. "And any second now,
he'll realise..."

"I'm stuck!" the goblin howled
suddenly. "They've tricked me!"

"Perfect timing," chuckled Cherry.

The goblin was stuck fast, unable
to move his feet in the super-sticky
icing. Rachel laughed out loud at his
furious face. "Brilliant idea, Kirsty,"
she cheered.

Cherry flew over to the goblin, her eyes on her precious party bag, but he bared his teeth at her. "Any closer, fairy, and I'll bite you!" he warned.

"In that case, I'll have to take you back to Fairyland," Cherry said calmly. "And won't the Fairy Godmother be interested to hear what you and Jack Frost have been plotting?"

The goblin scowled, but said no more.

"Serves you right for ruining my cake – twice!" Kirsty couldn't help adding.

"Don't worry about your cake,

Kirsty," Cherry said. "Once I've got my party bag back, I'll magic you the most beautiful birthday cake you've ever seen. Now, I don't suppose you two would like to come to Fairyland with me, would you?"

"Yes, please!" Kirsty cried at once, but Rachel was glancing up at the kitchen clock.

"What about your party, Kirsty?" she pointed out. "Musical Statues must be about to end soon."

Cherry twirled her wand around. "Don't worry," she said, "I'll work some magic so that it will seem as if you've only been gone from the party for a moment. Will that help?"

"Oh, yes!" cried both girls together.

"I was hoping you'd say that," Cherry smiled. "Off we go!"

A Magical Mystery Cake!

With a blur of bright colours – and the delicious smell of freshly baked cakes – Kirsty and Rachel found themselves whizzing through the air towards Fairyland.

"Hello," they heard a sweet voice calling as they landed with a bump. "Which one of you is Kirsty and which one is Rachel? I've heard so much about you, my dears."

Kirsty and Rachel blinked and looked around. They were back in Fairyland, and were now fairy-sized themselves. And there, standing in front of them, was somebody who could only be the Fairy Godmother. She had long copper hair swept up into a ponytail, the kindest green eyes that Rachel and Kirsty had ever seen, and wings that shimmered

every time they moved. Her long
golden dress was covered in tiny
glimmering jewels that twinkled with
all the colours of the rainbow.

"I'm Kirsty," Kirsty said, jumping
up at once.

"And I'm Rachel," Rachel added,
scrambling to her feet.

"Delighted to meet you at last,"
the Fairy Godmother replied,
dropping a beautiful curtsey.

Then her eyes narrowed at
the sight of the goblin,
standing next
to Cherry. "I see
that you've taken
something that
doesn't belong to
you," she said sternly,
pointing a
finger at Cherry's
party bag.
Whizz! The
party bag glowed
with red and
purple light and
shot out of the
goblin's hands at once.
It zoomed straight over to
Cherry, who clutched it with relief.
"Thank you!" she cried.
"You're welcome, my dear," the
Fairy Godmother said. Then she

fixed her gaze on the goblin. "As for you, I've got just the thing to teach you a lesson." She pointed a finger at him. "You'll need that," she said, "and that." Kirsty and Rachel couldn't help laughing as an enormous chef's hat suddenly appeared on the goblin's head, and a crisp white apron wrapped itself around his body.

"You can help in the Party Workshop for the rest of the week, icing all the cakes," the Fairy Godmother went on firmly. "Let's hope that keeps you out of mischief."

The goblin looked very sulky as Cherry bustled him away. "You won't catch the other goblins so easily," he snarled. "We'll get the rest of those party bags, just you wait and see!"

Once he'd gone, the Fairy Godmother turned back to Kirsty and Rachel. "I'm afraid he might be right," she told them. "Jack Frost's goblins can be very cunning, as you know. They'll try every trick they can think of to steal the other magical party bags."

"What can we do to help?" Kirsty asked at once.

The Fairy Godmother smiled and sighed. "All you can do is look out for trouble at parties," she said. "The goblins are likely to try and spoil human parties because they know that the Party Fairies will rush to help.

That will give them the chance they need to steal the fairies' party bags."

"We'll keep a look-out," Rachel promised.

At that moment, Cherry returned. "We'd better send you back to your party," she told the girls. "And don't worry – I'm sure there won't be any more goblins to spoil your fun today." She carefully opened her party bag and reached inside. Then, just as the Fairy Godmother pointed her wand at the girls and called, "Home!" Cherry threw a handful of red and purple fairy dust over them.

The world seemed to spin, there was a sweet, sugary smell in

the air and then the girls found
themselves back in Kirsty's kitchen.

"Jessica's the winner!" they heard
Mrs Tate saying. "Come and get
your prize for being the best statue,
Jessica."

"It sounds like the game's only just
finished," Kirsty said happily. "Just
like Cherry promised. Let's go and
join the party again, Rachel."

But Rachel was staring at the

kitchen table in wonder. "Look, Kirsty!" she gulped. "Look at your cake!"

Kirsty gasped in surprise. The red and purple fairy dust that Cherry had thrown over them was floating down onto the cake that Mr Tate had made. As the girls watched, they realised that the fairy dust was actually red and purple hundreds and thousands, and as they landed on the cake something amazing happened. A delicious fragrance of vanilla and sugar

floated around the room, and the
original cake melted into thin air,
while a new cake formed in its
place. Kirsty and Rachel
stared in wonder as
three tiers appeared,
one by one,
beautifully
covered with
white, pink and
lilac icing. Each
tier was
decorated with
tiny sugar fairies,
twining sugar
roses and shiny
silver bells.
Kirsty broke the
silence with a sudden laugh.
"It's the Party Fairies!" she cried,
pointing at the sugar figures.
"There's Cherry with a wooden

59

spoon, see? And the Glitter Fairy, didn't Bertram say her name was Grace? And a fairy with a present – that must be Jasmine. And –"

Suddenly, they heard Mrs Tate calling for them. "Kirsty! Rachel! Where are you?"

"Time to go," Rachel said. "Shall we take the cake in with us, just to be on the safe side?"

"Good idea," said Kirsty. Then she grinned. "I can't wait to see everybody's faces!"

Very carefully, the girls lifted the magnificent cake. As they carried it into the living room together, the little silver bells tinkled merrily.

"Wow!" cried Kirsty's friend Jessica. "I've never seen anything like it."

Another girl, Molly, was licking her lips. "It's almost too beautiful to eat," she said. "Although it smells so gorgeous, I'll give it a try!"

Mrs Tate looked dazzled. "It's a work of art!" she said to her husband in amazement.

Mr Tate was staring at the cake, too, with a bewildered expression on his face. "Well... Um... It's not so difficult when you know how," he said sheepishly.

"I can't wait to see what you're going to do for my birthday next month!" Mrs Tate added. Mr Tate looked rather alarmed at that, so

Kirsty interrupted quickly. "Shall we cut the cake, Mum?"

"Good idea," Mrs Tate replied. She lit the candles, and everybody sang 'Happy Birthday'. Then Kirsty carefully sliced into the lowest tier of the cake. As she did so, hundreds of magical butterflies fluttered out into the room, their colourful wings sparkling in the sunshine.

"Ooooh!" everybody exclaimed, as the butterflies vanished into thin air. "Just like magic!"

Kirsty and Rachel smiled at each other. They both knew that it magic – fairy magic, the most wonderful magic in all the world!

As they tucked into slices of the delicious birthday cake, they both thought of their new fairy mission with excitement.

"I can't wait to meet the other Party Fairies," Rachel whispered to Kirsty. "But I'm not looking forward to seeing any more goblins."

"I know," Kirsty agreed. "I just hope we can stop them from spoiling the King and Queen's party."

Rachel patted her friend's arm comfortingly. "At least Cherry said there'd be no more trouble at your party," she pointed out. "So we can enjoy the rest of your birthday without worrying."

Kirsty nodded. "Yes," she said. Then she grinned. "An invitation to the King and Queen's jubilee party, meeting Cherry and a visit to Fairyland – I just knew this was going to be a wonderful birthday," she sighed happily, "and I was right."